Please Please the BEES

Gerald Kelley

Albert Whitman & Company
Chicago, Illinois

For Richard

Library of Congress Cataloging-in-Publication Data

Names: Kelley, Gerald, author, illustrator.
Title: Please please the bees / Gerald Kelley.
Description: Chicago, Illinois : Albert Whitman and Company, 2017.
Summary: Accustomed to the daily jars of honey provided by the bees living in his yard,
Benedict the bear is upset when they go on strike, but he listens to their requests for
better working conditions and makes an effort to please the unhappy bees.
Identifiers: LCCN 2017010793 | ISBN 978-0-8075-5183-7 (hardback)
Subjects: | CYAC: Bees—Fiction. | Bears—Fiction. | Honey—Fiction. | Strikes and lockouts—Fiction.
BISAC: JUVENILE FICTION / Animals / Insects, Spiders, etc..
Classification: LCC PZ7.1.K4197 Pl 2017 | DDC [E]—dc23
LC record available at https://lccn.loc.gov/2017010793

Printed in China
10 9 8 7 6 5 4 3 2 LP 22 21 20 19 18 17

Design by Jordan Kost

For more information about Albert Whitman & Company,
visit our website at www.albertwhitman.com.

Benedict was a creature of habit.
  He liked to do the same thing every day.
  Every morning he woke up at the same time.
  Every morning he stretched. He scratched.
He yawned a great yawn.

Every morning the
bees delivered three
jars full of honey.

Benedict ate the same breakfast he'd eaten since he was just a fuzzy cub: toast with honey and tea with extra honey.

Next came his daily routine:

practicing,

perfecting his honey cake recipe,

knitting,

and running errands.

At night he'd read
then have one last cup
of honey tea before bed.
Life was sweet.

Until one morning...
One morning things
weren't the same.
In fact, something
terribly un-same
had happened.

There was no more honey.
The bees had gone on strike!

Benedict's breakfast wasn't the same without honey.

Without his honey tea, he couldn't knit.

Practice was dreadful.

He didn't even bother
with the errands.

Benedict became deeply discouraged.

Just then he heard someone say, "Hey, you! In the fur coat!"
It was a very small bee with a remarkably loud voice.
"We need to talk!" said the bee.

"Talk? Hmmph!" grumbled Benedict. "I let you all live in my yard. All I ask is for a few jars of honey. You should be grateful. Not go on strike!"

"A few jars?" said the bee.
"Buddy, we deliver three jars
of honey to you every day.
Every month! Every year!
Do the math, Einstein!"

"The hive is a wreck!" the bee continued. "It's all we can do to keep the walls from falling in! The roof leaks. Wind blows through the cracks. The last three queens up and quit on us because of the lousy working conditions."

The bee showed Benedict the garden. "Look!" the bee said. "Weeds everywhere. We have to fly miles away just to find enough flowers to make our honey. So we voted to strike."

"You're taking us for granted," the bee declared. "You want honey? Things need to change. It's up to you, bear."

And with that, the very small bee flew off.

The thought of losing his honey sent a chill down Benedict's spine. He had a lot to think about.

"Maybe I've been too selfish," Benedict said to himself. "I never thought about what the bees need. But how am I going to make this right?"

So he did some research.

He did a little shopping.

And he did a lot of work.

Benedict even learned how to harvest honey.
"I suppose it's a bit rude to expect them to do it
all themselves," he thought.

Finally, he was ready to show the bees all the work he'd done.

What would they think? He held his breath as he waited.

Then he heard the remarkably loud voice of the very small bee...

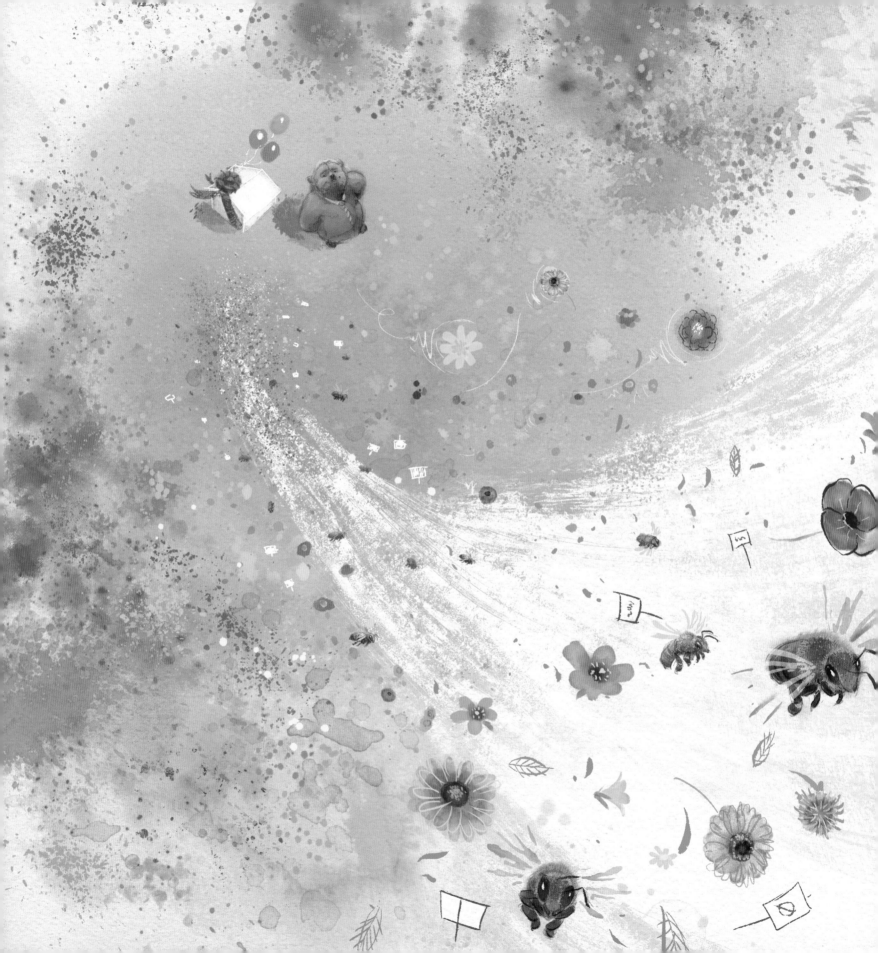

"DROP THE SIGNS,
GIRLS! TIME TO GET
BACK TO WORK!"

These days, Benedict is still
a creature of habit.
He still has his daily routine,
but he doesn't take the honey
for granted anymore.
He knows his life is sweet...

but now it's even sweeter...

for everyone.